April Fool!
Watch Out at School!

Diane deGroat

HARPERCOLLINS*PUBLISHERS*

April Fool! Watch Out at School!
Copyright © 2009 by Diane deGroat
Manufactured in China.

Library of Congress Cataloging-in-Publication Data is available.
ISBN 978-0-06-143042-8 (trade bdg.) — ISBN 978-0-06-143043-5 (lib. bdg.)

Typography by Jeanne L. Hogle
1 2 3 4 5 6 7 8 9 10
❖
First Edition

Have you found all the tricks in the illustrations?

Cover: One of the jokers is Gilbert. *Pages 2–3:* On the calendar, April has 31 days; one of the stars on the pajamas is Gilbert. *Pages 4–5:* One sneaker is red and one is blue; the clock says Gilbert gets up at 11:00; the calendar says that April has 31 days. *Pages 6–7:* The steering wheel is on the wrong side of the bus; students are going in the EXIT door; there are valentines on the windows in April; the sign in front of the school says TOWN POOL. *Pages 8–9:* The clock is backward; the writing on the board is upside down; Patty is reading a music book; there is a fork in Mrs. Byrd's pencil holder. *Pages 10–11:* Lewis's name is spelled wrong. *Page 12:* The writing on the board is backward. *Page 13:* Gilbert is spelled wrong. *Pages 14–15:* A sign on the wall says MARS; Mrs. Byrd's picture is on a lunch box; the duck's pants are on backward. *Pages 16–17:* The raccoon is eating a shoe; there is an alien sitting in the back row; Patty has two different-colored shoes. *Page 18:* Gilbert has an extra finger on his hand. *Page 19:* Gilbert is missing his glasses. *Pages 20–21:* Lewis is wearing a blue shirt. *Pages 22–23:* Lewis is kicking a bowling ball. *Page 24:* The stripes on Gilbert's shirt are vertical. *Page 25:* Mrs. Byrd is wearing overalls. *Page 26:* There's an elephant in the room. *Page 27:* The kids are painting Christmas pictures. *Pages 28–29:* N and M are switched on the alphabet poster; the globe is upside down; Margaret is reading *Goodnight Sun* instead of *Goodnight Moon*; George Washington is wearing earrings; George Washington is also Diane deGroat! *Page 30:* Nothing wrong. *Page 31:* Lewis is missing his shoes. *Page 32:* Lewis is missing one shoe.

Other Books About Gilbert

Mother, You're the Best! (But Sister, You're a Pest!)
Last One in Is a Rotten Egg!
No More Pencils, No More Books, No More Teacher's Dirty Looks!
Brand-new Pencils, Brand-new Books
We Gather Together...Now Please Get Lost!
Good Night, Sleep Tight, Don't Let the Bedbugs Bite!
Liar, Liar, Pants on Fire
Happy Birthday to You, You Belong in a Zoo
Jingle Bells, Homework Smells
Roses Are Pink, Your Feet Really Stink
Trick or Treat, Smell My Feet

Gilbert woke up and looked at the calendar. It was April 1st—April Fools' Day! He hopped out of bed and started filling his backpack with tricks to play on his friends.

His sister, Lola, peeked in the door and said, "Knock, knock."

Gilbert answered, "Who's there?"

"April Fool!" Lola shouted.

Gilbert laughed and explained, "You're supposed to play a trick on someone. Not tell jokes!"

"Okay," Lola said. "Do a trick on me." But Gilbert didn't have time to play tricks on his little sister. He was already out the door.

Gilbert met Patty on the corner. As they walked to school, Patty suddenly said, "Watch out, Gilbert—your shoe's untied!"

Gilbert stopped to tie his shoe, but it was already tied.

"Gotcha!" Patty said. "April Fool!"

Gilbert laughed. He couldn't wait to try that trick on someone else!

Principal Pug smiled and waved when he saw them. "Morning good," he said. "Day nice a have!" He was talking backward! The bell rang, and Patty said to Gilbert, "Up hurry let's!"

Mrs. Byrd was not smiling or waving. She said, "Put away your tricks so we can get started with our reading lesson. Gilbert, please start on page ten."

Gilbert stood up and read out loud: "'Where is my book?' Sam asked. 'I need it now!'"

Mrs. Byrd stopped him and said, "When someone reads out loud, it would be nice to know where the punctuation marks are." Then she said, "Here's an idea. When you come to a period, say 'POP,' and when you see quotation marks, say 'PHFFT.' A question mark can be 'HUH?' And the exclamation point is a 'BOING.' Try it."

Gilbert took a deep breath and started over. "PHFFT where is my book HUH? PHFFT Sam asked POP PHFFT I need it now BOING— Whew!" Gilbert said. "This is hard!"

Lewis said, "And it sure is funny—BOING!"

Everyone laughed. Mrs. Byrd laughed too and said, "Thank you for being such a good sport, Gilbert. April Fool!"

Gilbert sat down and made a loud PLFFTT sound in his seat. "That wasn't me!" he cried. "Somebody put a whoopee cushion there!"

"Gotcha!" Lewis said.

They finished their reading silently, but Gilbert kept thinking
POP and BOING whenever he saw a period or an exclamation
point.

He also kept thinking about how he could play a trick on
Lewis. He had hot spicy gum in his pocket, so he turned to
Lewis and asked, "Would you like a piece of gum, Lewis?"

"No way," Lewis said.

Later Gilbert put a plastic spider on Lewis's desk when he wasn't looking. "This is so fake," Lewis said when he handed it back. Then he slapped Gilbert on the back and said, "Your tricks are the worst!"

But Gilbert wasn't giving up. He still had a few more tricks up his sleeve.

He also had a sign on his back that said, "I smell." No wonder everyone was snickering as he walked to the cafeteria.

"Lewis!" Gilbert grumbled.

Before he ate, Gilbert first checked his seat for a whoopee cushion. There was none, so he sat down and opened his lunch box. Suddenly he jumped out of his seat and yelled, "AGGGH!" There was a worm in his apple!

"It's just a gummy worm," Patty said. "And look—there's a note."

The note said, "April Fool!" It was signed "Mother." Gilbert couldn't believe it. Even his mother had tricked him!

At recess Frank said, "Watch out, Gilbert—there's a bee on your head!" Gilbert swatted at his head while Frank laughed and said, "April Fool!"

Margaret said, "Watch out, Gilbert! Your shoe's untied."

Gilbert bent to tie his shoe.

"Made you look!" Margaret said.

Gilbert sighed. He couldn't believe that he had fallen for that trick twice in one day!

Then Philip shouted, "Watch out, Gilbert!"

But Gilbert wasn't going to get tricked again! He said, "I'm not—" Before he could finish, a kick ball smacked him on the head.

"I told you to watch out," Philip said.

"I thought it was another trick." Gilbert groaned as he rubbed his head. "This is the worst April Fools' Day ever—everybody's playing tricks on me, but I can't trick anyone!"

"I told you your tricks were bad!" Lewis laughed. "You'll never trick anyone!"

Gilbert said, "That's what you think, Lewis. I have one more trick I've been saving just for you."

Lewis laughed again and said, "What is it?"

"I'm not telling you. You'll have to wait and see it."

Gilbert whispered to Patty what his trick was. Patty said loudly, "You're right, Gilbert. That's the best trick ever!"

Lewis snorted and said,
"You'll never April Fool me!"

As they walked back into the classroom, Gilbert said, "Oh, Lewis—let me hold that door for you."

Lewis asked, "Is this your trick?"

"No," said Gilbert. He held the door open, and Lewis walked through. Very quickly.

During spelling, Lewis couldn't find his eraser. Gilbert said, "Here, Lewis. You can borrow mine."

Lewis looked at the eraser and said, "Is this a trick?"

"No," Gilbert said. But Lewis inspected the eraser very carefully before he used it.

When they went to the art table, Gilbert pulled out a chair and said, "Here you go, Lewis—have a seat."

Lewis looked at the chair and said, "It's a trick, right?"

"No," Gilbert said. But Lewis checked the chair very carefully for a whoopee cushion before he sat down.

When Lewis got up to clean his brush, Gilbert said, "Be careful, Lewis—your shoe is untied!"

"Ha!" Lewis said. "I'm not falling for that old trick!"

But his shoe *was* untied. And Lewis *did* fall when he stepped on the lace. Everyone laughed.

"I told you it was untied," Gilbert said.

"I thought it was your trick," Lewis said, tying his shoe.

"No," Gilbert said. "My trick is much better than that!"

During quiet time, Gilbert brought a book to Lewis and said,
"I think you should read this, Lewis. I really liked it."

Lewis wouldn't take the book. He said, "Is it a fake book? Is it
glued shut? Is it going to squirt me when I open it?"

"No," Gilbert said. "It's just a really good book."

Lewis took the book, but he couldn't concentrate on the story.

He kept looking over his shoulder to see where Gilbert was.

Lewis was so busy watching out for Gilbert's trick, he didn't see Kenny putting a fake spider on his desk. Lewis screamed when he saw it. "Gotcha!" Kenny said.

And when Patty told Lewis his shoe was untied, he bent to tie it. "Gotcha!" Patty laughed.

And when Lewis sat on his own whoopee cushion and Margaret said, "Gotcha!" everyone laughed!

When the bell rang, Lewis finally shouted,

"I give up, Gilbert! I can't stand it anymore! Do your trick already!"

Gilbert smiled and said, "There isn't any trick, Lewis—I just made you think that there was! You got April Fooled!

"Gotcha!"